THE FIRST MARTIAN

Titles in Teen Reads:

Badger Publishing Limited, Oldmedow Road, Hardwick Industrial Estate, King's Lynn PE30 4JJ
Telephone: 01438 791037

www.badgerlearning.co.uk

THE FIRST MARTIAN

IAIN MCLAUGHLIN

Badger
LEARNING

The First Martian ISBN 978-1-78464-605-9

Publisher: Susan Ross
Senior Editor: Danny Pearson
Editorial Coordinator: Claire Morgan
Copyeditor: Cambridge Publishing Management
Designer: Bigtop Design Ltd
Cover: AF archive / Alamy Stock Photo

2 4 6 8 10 9 7 5 3 1

Freak.

Lucas knew he wasn't like the other students in his school.

Freak.

Lucas Wilson knew he was different.

Freak.

None of the others were famous the way he was.

Freak.

None of the others needed to wear a mechanical outer skeleton just to walk around every day.

Freak.

None of the others had been born on Mars.

Lucas *really* was a Martian. Nobody else at his school could say that. Actually, nobody else in the *world* could say that. He was unique. Lucas was the first human to be born on Mars. And so far, he was the *only* one ever to be born on Mars.

And most of the time he wished he was still there on that distant, red planet.

CHAPTER 1

INTO THE ARMOUR

"Lucas, you'll be late for school."

Lucas didn't need reminding that he was running late. He didn't need reminding that he was going to school either. School wasn't something he could forget about. He knew that for a fact because he had spent enough time trying to forget school. He tried to forget the other students and the way they looked at him. He tried to forget how heavy he felt and how tired he was even by lunchtime.

He tried to forget how much he missed home, how much he missed Mars. He really missed putting on his spacesuit and walking out onto the surface of Mars and exploring with his parents. He had loved the fact that he was going to places no human had ever been to before. On Earth, everybody had seen everything before.

"Lucas?" His mother's voice again.

"I'm nearly ready," Lucas called. And that was nearly true. He was showered and dressed, and he had carefully strapped himself into the Armour. That was the name he had given the mechanical skeleton he had to put on every morning. This time he was wearing it differently. This time he had strapped it *under* his clothes. The Armour was made of reinforced metal rods and panels that ran the length of his arms and legs. It gave them extra strength and it supported Lucas's spine. The Armour had been designed to go on top of a pair of jeans and a shirt. With the Armour out of sight under his clothes, Lucas smiled. Maybe if he just *looked* normal, things would be easier?

But even as he stood up from his bed, he could feel something was wrong. He felt the metal sliding against his skin. It felt *wrong*. The Armour wasn't giving the support he needed. His leg twisted inside the metal frame and his back jerked to try to keep his balance. A second later Lucas hit the floor hard.

"Lucas?"

Lucas heard the worry in his mother's voice, followed by her hurried footsteps. His bedroom door opened and his mother looked at him. The concern on her face was clear.

"I fell," he said before his mother could speak.

His mother sat on his bed and she helped him up until he was sitting beside her. Sometimes Lucas forgot that his mum was still getting used to Earth's higher gravity too. She didn't have the strength to just lift him to his feet. "Where's the Armour?" Mum asked.

Lucas pulled up the leg of his trousers to show the metal frame. "I thought..." his voice tailed off into a miserable silence.

His mum put an arm around Lucas's shoulders and she pulled him into a hug. He called it her Mum-hug. She was going to tell him something he didn't like but she wanted him to know she loved him. "You thought if nobody saw the exo-skeleton you could fit in a bit more easily?" Mum was a scientist. Like every scientist she *loved* big words. "Exo-skeleton" was her official name for the Armour.

"Yeah," Lucas nodded. "They all look at me like I'm a..." He had been about to say 'freak'. But the word hurt so much when other people said it. He didn't want to say it out loud himself. "They just look at me like I'm weird and different."

"I'm sorry, kiddo," Mum said with sympathy. "A lot of them are just jealous that you've seen another planet."

"They call me an alien," Lucas said miserably.

Mum brushed a stray lock of hair out of Lucas's eye. "All of them?"

"No," Lucas admitted. "Just the popular ones who run the school."

"The teachers run the school," Mum corrected him quickly. "And those popular kids probably used to get all the attention. I bet they're envious. They don't like it that you're more interesting than they are."

"I don't want attention," Lucas said softly. "I just want…" He stopped, wondering exactly what he *did* want. He knew what he didn't want. He *didn't* want to go to school.

Mum squeezed his shoulders again. "You have friends," she said comfortingly.

That was true. Jess Raymond and Danny Arthur were the best friends he had. They were probably the *only* friends he had but they were funny and supportive. Most days they were what got him through school. However, Lucas was in such a sour mood today that he didn't want to admit to anything good. "Only two."

"You'll make more friends," Mum promised. She stood. Lucas could see that it took effort for her to stand. "But not if you sit here all day. Now put your Armour on top of your clothes. It wasn't designed to be worn next to your skin. Then get dressed and we'll get you to school."

Mum left the room and Lucas started pulling miserably at his shirt.

***

Lucas arrived at his school with only a few minutes to spare before the start of class. Harringden was a private school where all the students came from wealthy and fortunate backgrounds. Most of them had amazingly rich parents. Politicians, solicitors, businesspeople… they even had a duke's son and daughter enrolled at the school. Lucas's parents were pretty well-off. They had made good money from their adventures on Mars. The strange thing was that they were probably the most normal family with a pupil at this school — even though they had lived on another planet for a decade. The truth was that they had chosen Harringden as the school for Lucas *because* it had so many children from wealthy and important families. The school had experience in keeping its pupils away from the snooping eyes of the media. It had a reputation for having the best security of any school in Britain.

When Lucas and his parents had arrived back on Earth they had been celebrities. His parents had travelled to Mars as part of a large international science experiment. They had been due to stay on the Red Planet for eighteen months. They lived in Habitats, which had been built by 3D printers sent across space to Mars a few years ahead of them. The printers had done their job well. They built the domed Habitats from materials they drew from the Martian soil. They had also built a series of scientific domes. One of those had a greenhouse made of sheets of hardwearing transparent plastic. It had been brought from Earth along with the printers and the solar panels they used for power. The mission and all its preparations had run very smoothly. In fact, there had only been one small, unexpected surprise in the whole mission.

Lucas's mother had become pregnant.

There was no way she could travel back to Earth before the baby was born. Travel between the planets was only possible when the orbits of the two worlds brought them close. Doctors were clear that giving birth in space in zero gravity was not an option either. So she had to stay behind on Mars to have her baby. The pressures of lifting off from a planet's surface put a great deal of stress on a human body. A baby or young child would never survive the gravity produced during a blast-off. That meant that Lucas and his family had stayed on Mars until he was ten years old before finally returning home.

They had lived comfortably in their Habitats, acting as pioneers on this distant world and as caretakers of the Habitats. They kept the buildings operational for the various scientific teams who joined them every eighteen months or so. They had also overseen the 3D printers as the busy little machines built more and more Habitats and expanded the scientific sections of the colony. They had been there while the colony had grown into a real community. When Lucas was four years old, a group of twelve scientists had arrived from Earth to begin work on colonising Mars permanently. They were supposed to be the first humans to have long stays on Mars, withmore to follow in later missions.

***

Lucas and his parents had beaten them to it. The scientists hadn't minded one bit. In fact, they had gained a huge amount of valuable information from Lucas's parents. For Lucas, these newcomers became an extended family of aunts and uncles. They had brought him toys from Earth. Most of all, they had brought *themselves*. They were the first people he had really talked to apart from his parents. None of them objected to him being around and they all made time to talk with him and answer his questions. In return, Lucas showed them the best places in the Habitats to watch the Sun set behind a far-off range of mountains. He also took them to the best place to listen when a sandstorm passed over the colony. They were his family and his friends. He had cried when he realised that he would have to leave them behind on Mars. Even now he still missed them.

The journey to Earth was boring. It was six months trapped in a small spacecraft in zero gravity. Being able to float soon lost any interest for Lucas. Every day was exactly the same in the spaceship. Lucas had lessons in the morning and afternoon. Three times a day he had to exercise hard. He needed to build his muscles so that they would work on Earth. His parents kept repeating that Earth's gravity was nearly three times stronger than it had been back on Mars. It would be much harder for Lucas to move around on Earth.

It all made Lucas wonder why his parents wanted to go back to Earth. It also made him afraid of this strange planet they were heading towards. Would he be able to move around at all? Would he have to stay in a chair all day, every day? On top of that, Lucas didn't know anyone on Earth. His parents would be the only people on the whole planet that he knew.

During the long, boring journey through space, Lucas really became afraid of Earth and that fear slowly turned to a kind of terrified hatred.

The horrible thing was that Earth was far worse than he had expected.

CHAPTER 2

FRIENDS AND ENEMIES

As soon as his spaceship had landed, Lucas could feel the Earth's gravity pressing down on him. His parents had made him work hard to build his muscles when they were on Mars. In fact, Lucas had really enjoyed doing the exercises. They had been like a game, and the scientists had taken turns in helping. But despite all his hard work, Lucas's muscles still weren't strong enough for Earth. That meant he had to wear the skeleton of metal panels and rods he called the Armour. That had caught the interest of the media, who wanted to know everything about the boy they had named 'The First Martian'. He was the only alien on Earth. To them, that meant he was a news story, not a person. NASA and the UK Government had done all they could to protect Lucas and his family — Lucas in particular. But some journalists showed they were unwilling to follow the rules, and that had made Harringden's security more appealing. Unfortunately, although Harringden kept Lucas safe from the outside world, it couldn't protect him from the other pupils.

If Lucas was being fair about Harringden, he would have admitted that the teachers tried really hard to defend him from the other students. He was just sorry that he needed to be protected. On Mars he hadn't needed any protection.

As usual, Lucas found Jess and Danny waiting for him when he arrived at Harringden. Jess's bright red hair made her stand out in a crowd, easy for him to see. It also made her easy prey for idiots with insults. "Carrot-top" and "Satsuma" were just two of the names she was called. Danny was tall and skinny and he was usually close enough to Jess to be spotted quickly enough. They both smiled broadly as Lucas walked across a stretch of grass to the bench where they were sitting. Seeing them lifted Lucas's spirits.

"Hiya," Jess said brightly.

"No luck with getting the Armour under your clothes, then?" Danny asked. That was typical of Danny. Being tactful wasn't his talent in life.

Lucas thumped an angry fist on the wide metal panel running up his thigh. "It wouldn't work," he explained. There was a mechanical rasp from the knee joints of the exo-skeleton as Lucas sat down on the bench. "It doesn't get a proper grip against my skin."

"I'm sorry," Danny said. "I know you wanted rid of the Armour."

"You wasted your time sitting down," Jess said, standing. She was pointing at the school's main door. A young woman of around thirty was standing looking out at the students. "Miss

Cotton's out — that means the bell will go any time now."

Sure enough, the bell rang out loudly across the school grounds. Lucas's Armour wheezed as he rose to his feet. The walk along the school drive had tired his legs and he thought about increasing the power in the Armour. It had twelve power settings and Lucas usually kept it on three, the third lowest. When he had started at Harringden, his default setting had been five. Lucas knew that he had to increase his muscle strength to deal with Earth's gravity. He also knew that would never happen if he relied on the Armour to do everything. He had reduced the power by two settings in just a few months. He resisted the urge to increase the setting to four, and with Jess and Danny started walking towards the front door. Despite assistance from the Armour, they were still overtaken by most of the other students on their way into the school building. As usual, some of the less pleasant pupils had something to say as they passed.

"Hurry up, alien." It was James Gossford. His mother was some kind of big-time businesswoman and his father was a politician. Lucas had never bothered listening to which party Gossford's father belonged to. He didn't care. James Gossford was vile enough without thinking about what sort of horrible parents he must have. Besides, politics was the most boring thing Lucas had ever come across. On Mars there hadn't been any politics.

It was Jess who answered. "Shut up, Gossford," she snapped.

Gossford just sneered. "Calm down, Carrot-top. Can't your boyfriend speak for himself?" A really nasty expression appeared on the boy's face. "Or does he only speak Martian?"

"That's enough!"

Gossford spun around. Miss Cotton was standing behind him. She had heard everything and she didn't look happy. "Miss... I..."

"You've been warned about picking on other students, James." Miss Cotton scribbled on a pad and tore off the top sheet, handing it to Gossford. "That's detention for every break today. Next time it will be for a full week."

"But…" Gossford's shoulder slumped. Harringden was old-fashioned in many of its traditions. That meant once a detention was handed out it was never taken back. "Come on," he said sulkily to his friends. They all went inside miserably.

Miss Cotton smiled at Lucas. "You won't have to worry about him today anyway."

Lucas smiled gratefully. "Thanks." Miss Cotton had always been good to him. She had kept an eye out for the other students picking on him. He knew there would be some kind of revenge from Gossford at some point but it wouldn't be today and he was thankful for that. He liked Miss Cotton and he liked her boyfriend, Mr Skinner, the chemistry teacher, too. They were young and fun. More than that they were both fair to him and treated him like everybody else.

"In you go," Miss Cotton called, hurrying them inside. "If you're late *I'll* get detention."

***

That particular morning at Harringden wasn't too bad. It was definitely better than many mornings Lucas had experienced at school. After registration there was an hour and a half of English. That was all right because it was Miss Cotton's class. She kept things moving along quickly and she always tried to keep a happy atmosphere in her lessons. Morning break was brightened by the lack of Gossford. As Danny cheerfully pointed out, Gossford could improve any situation just by not being there. The rest of the morning was split between maths and the start of a chemistry lesson that would finish in the afternoon. English interested Lucas. Growing up on Mars, he had had very limited access to children's movies and TV. But there were plenty of books. By the time he was ten, Lucas had read hundreds of books, from children's favourites through to literary classics. In truth, he had found most of the so-called 'classics' hard work. The style was too wordy and some of the plots were slow. However, he had a stubborn streak that made him finish even the dustiest old classic. Having grown up with only scientists for company, Lucas knew maths and all the sciences very well. In truth, the lessons at school were far too easy for him. But he enjoyed them anyway and his test scores were always very, very good.

The first hint that something would spoil the morning came when Miss Cotton entered Mr Skinner's science class. There were some giggles and a few whistles and catcalls. Everyone knew that Miss Cotton and Mr Skinner were a couple. It was obvious in the way they looked at each other. The two teachers spoke in low voices for a moment before Mr Skinner looked at Lucas.

"Lucas, could Miss Cotton see you in the corridor for a minute, please?"

There was a low rumble of conversation among the students. A few called out that Lucas must be in trouble. He ignored the comments.

Lucas followed Miss Cotton out into the corridor and she pulled the door closed behind them. She looked a bit worried. "Lucas, do you know anything about a doctor coming to see you today?"

"No." That was the first Lucas had heard of another doctor's appointment. For months after he arrived on Earth doctors had poked and prodded at him. They had taken more blood than he even thought could fit into his body. They had also put him through hour after hour of tiring and stupid tests. Most of them hadn't bothered to explain to him what the tests were for. His parents always gave him as much information as they could, and he had heard them shouting at some of the doctors about the way they treated Lucas. The problem was that he had to see so many different doctors. There was always a new one to annoy him. He was sick of doctors and he didn't want to see another one. "Mum didn't mention it."

Miss Cotton bit her lip worriedly. "She didn't mention it to us either. That's not like her."

That was certainly true. Lucas's mum was careful about details. It was part of her training as a scientist. Forgetting to tell anyone about a doctor's appointment just wasn't like her. Something else struck Lucas as odd. "Why is the doctor coming here? If I have to see a doctor I usually have to go to London or wherever they are."

"That struck us as odd as well," Miss Cotton said. "I think we should phone your mum. What do you think?"

Lucas nodded. "Definitely."

They hurried to the school's office as fast as Lucas could walk. Unfortunately, neither the telephone nor the video messenger link-ups in the school office were working.

"Sorry, Miss Cotton," Mrs Gardner, the school secretary said. "The school's cable connection is down. All of our phones go through it. The internet as well. I've had teachers down here complaining for the last ten minutes. I thought that was why you were here."

"Not really," Miss Cotton answered. "We were going to call Lucas's mum. Never mind. We'll use my mobile phone."

Miss Cotton led Lucas to the staff room. "First time in here?" She asked Lucas as she opened a locker.

"Yeah," Lucas answered, looking around. The room was disappointingly dull. It had a number of chairs and sofas scattered around, with a large TV screen in the corner. One wall had a small kitchen area and another wall held the lockers where the teachers put their bags and coats during the day. "I mean, yes, Miss Cotton."

The teacher smiled. "I'll let you off this time." Her smile faded and was replaced by a frown. "There isn't any signal," she said.

"We could try my phone," Lucas said.

"OK," Miss Cotton agreed. "And I hope your phone is in your locker. You know Mrs Bryant's rules. Everybody has to lock their phones away during the day, even the teachers."

Lucas smiled. "I know. It's not a popular rule."

They went back to the hall where the students' lockers were. Lucas opened his and found his phone. It didn't take long to find his mum in the contact list. He didn't have many friends. There were only eight contacts on his list, and two of those were emergency numbers for his doctors in London. He didn't use his phone much. He really only carried it because Mum and Dad insisted. "Got it," Lucas said, holding his phone up.

"Good," Miss Cotton said. "Do you want to phone your mum or would you prefer me to do it?"

"Maybe you should talk to her." Lucas pressed the button to dial his mum and was about to hand the phone over when an exclamation mark appeared on the screen with NO SIGNAL underneath. He showed it to Miss Cotton.

The teacher looked at his screen for a moment. "No signal," she read softly, "and you're on a different network from me."

"Am I?" Lucas asked.

Miss Cotton nodded. "So that means what?"

Lucas thought for a second. "That it's not just one network that's affected?" he asked.

"Spot on," Miss Cotton said. "Come on. I think we should tell Mrs Bryant about this, don't you?"

Mrs Bryant was sitting in her office when Lucas and Miss Cotton knocked at her door. She looked relieved at the distraction from the pile of papers on her desk. Miss Cotton quickly explained everything that had happened. Mrs Bryant looked worried and led Miss Cotton and Lucas to the school technician's office. Jon Daly, who was the school's IT technician, thought about the problem for a moment.

"It could be something really simple," Daly suggested. "Most of our communications go through a single point. We call that a hub."

Mrs Bryant was not a tall woman. She was short and slim but she had a big personality, a sharp brain and a warm smile. They all worked together to give her a real sense of authority. "Mr Daly, I know what a hub is."

"Is it likely that a hub's failure could kill all of our communications?" From her expression it was clear that Miss Cotton wasn't convinced by that explanation.

Neither was Mrs Bryant. "It's too much of a coincidence that this happens when we get that message about Lucas," the Head said. "And I don't believe in coincidences."

Mr Daly fished a set of car keys from his pocket. "I could nip into the village and find out what's happening. That's where our local hub is."

"Please do that," the Head agreed. "But go to the police station first. Find out if they know anything about what has happened." She picked up a pen from Mr Daly's untidy desk and quickly wrote a number on a sheet of paper. "This is the phone number of Lucas's mother. Call her while you're at the police station. Ask her if she knows about the doctor coming to see Lucas here at school today."

"Got it," Daly said, hurrying for the door.

The Head smiled a tight smile at Lucas. "It's probably nothing."

They all knew she was lying.

CHAPTER 3
THE LONELIEST BOY IN THE WORLD

Mrs Bryant tried to get things back to normal. "Go back to class, Lucas. If there's any kind of problem we'll deal with it."

Miss Cotton led Lucas back to Mr Skinner's classroom. "I bet it's the press up to their tricks," Miss Cotton muttered. "Could be that American tabloid again." The last time the *Independent Reporter* magazine had tried to get a picture of Lucas they had hacked the school's security system. They had set off the fire alarm so that the school had to be evacuated. Then they had managed to grab some pictures of Lucas lagging behind other pupils as they left the school. Of course, the magazine had edited the picture to make it look really terrible. All of the students behind Lucas were cut out along with the teachers who were hurrying them along. It looked as if Lucas had been abandoned. The magazine had taken a beating in the other media for its headline 'The Loneliest Boy in the World'. They didn't care. That picture had trebled their sales for that issue. Nobody at the school wanted another visit from them. Unfortunately, everyone expected the magazine to try again.

"I'm not that interesting," Lucas grumbled. "Why don't the papers leave me alone?"

Miss Cotton patted his shoulder kindly. "Because some of them are real… low-lifes." It sounded as if the teacher had only just stopped herself from calling them something much worse.

That thought made Lucas laugh. Miss Cotton was probably the politest person he had ever met. The thought of her calling someone a rude name was quite funny somehow.

By the time Lucas was back in his seat and Miss Cotton had spoken quietly to Mr Skinner, there were only a few minutes left until lunch break. The bell sounded for lunch before the lesson really got underway again.

"Well," Danny asked as soon as they were outside the classroom. "What was that all about?"

"Yep," Jess added. "Spill the beans."

With Danny on one side and Jess on the other, Lucas knew he had no chance to avoid talking about his trip out of the class. His friends looked both curious and concerned. "Somebody got in touch with the school saying a doctor was coming to see me here," Lucas said. "The Head and Miss Cotton think it's another scam by journalists to get pictures of 'The Loneliest Boy in the World'".

Jess looked fit to explode. "That's horrible," she said angrily.

"Totally," Danny agreed.

"They should be thrown into jail for this sort of thing," Jess snarled. "They've got no right to treat anybody this way."

"Well, they're out of luck," Lucas said firmly.

"How do you mean?" Jess asked.

Lucas swung his backpack onto his shoulder and turned towards the school's side door. "Because I'm not going to be here when they arrive." He headed for the door. "It's a sunny day. I'm going to have my lunch in the woods."

"We're not supposed to go off the school grounds," Danny reminded him.

Lucas shrugged. He didn't care. "I'm an alien. I forget things like that." Pushing the door open, Lucas hurried outside.

Jess and Danny exchanged helpless looks and then rushed after their friend. The woods were about two hundred metres from the school, on the other side of one of the playing fields. The school grounds were empty and nobody saw them disappear into the trees. The path through the woods twisted for a few hundred metres over rough ground. Lucas had to be careful when the ground was uneven. When the Armour was turned down to three his balance was a little shaky. The path led towards a small clearing beside a stream. In the middle of the clearing were some tree stumps that were the right height for sitting on. It was just close enough to the school for Lucas to walk there and just far away enough that nobody would find them. It was the perfect picnic spot for the three friends.

Settling down on the stumps, Lucas and his friends pulled their lunches from their bags and started eating.

Had Lucas or his friends been at the school at that moment they would have seen a large white van trundling along the drive towards the school's front door. A black car followed behind it and pulled up to the side of the van. A woman of around thirty, with short blonde hair, got out of the car and headed for the door, where the Head and Miss Cotton were already waiting.

"I'm Doctor Russell," the woman said, extending her hand to the Head. Mrs Bryant shook it without enthusiasm. "Please, call me Jasmine," the newcomer added with a friendly smile.

"You may call me Mrs Bryant, I'm the Head Teacher at Harringden," the Head replied coolly. She indicated the young teacher by her side. "This is Miss Cotton."

"A pleasure," Doctor Russell said, still smiling broadly. She seemed unaware of the cold way Miss Cotton kept their handshake so brief. "I really hope we haven't put you to too much trouble."

Mrs Bryant smiled thinly. "The local communications being out have caused us more trouble," she said. "Have you heard anything about that?"

"Did that hit you, too?" Russell shook her head. "We thought we had just driven into some local dead area for signal. We must have been lucky to get our call through to you."

"Very lucky," Miss Cotton replied quickly. "When we tried to contact Lucas's family about this all the communications were dead."

Russell looked surprised. "I spoke to Lucas's mum before we set off. I just caught her before she left for a meeting. It was something to do with farming and growing crops on alien worlds or something. Which crops grow well on Mars and which don't. It's probably really interesting but it sounded kind of dull to me." She looked sheepishly at her hosts. "There's a reason I'm a doctor not a farmer."

Neither teacher returned Russell's smile.

"What did Mrs Wilson say?" Mrs Bryant asked.

Russell coughed in embarrassment. "Well, she tore me apart for dropping this on her at the last minute. Actually," she corrected herself. "She tore me apart for dropping this on *Lucas* at the last minute."

Miss Cotton and Mrs Bryant exchanged a look that said they completely agreed with Lucas's mum.

***

Doctor Russell continued, "It's a really simple test that should have been done about three weeks ago, just to keep an eye on Lucas's progress. How his muscles are improving and how his lungs are coping with the extra workload. Things like that." She waved a hand in the direction of the white van. "Rather than drag Lucas into our labs we thought that we should bring the lab to him instead. Just to make it a bit easier for him." She looked a little uncomfortable. "Besides, it was our mistake, not his."

Mrs Bryant and Miss Cotton exchanged another long look before the Head finally nodded. "All right," she said. "That's if you have the proper passes and identification. But I don't appreciate one of my students having his schedule upset this way."

"And if you had warned us about this," Miss Cotton said sharply. "I'd have recommended against you bringing that thing to the school." She waved an angry hand at the van. "Lucas has a difficult enough time fitting in without you having that there to remind everyone that he's a bit different."

Russell looked to Mrs Bryant for some explanation of the teacher's outburst but found no support there.

"I agree completely with Miss Cotton," the Head said firmly. "And I assure you that I will not allow you to bring that van back here in future. However," she sniffed like there was a bad smell under her nose. "You're here now so you might as well get on with it and get it done."

"Excellent," Doctor Russell beamed.

"As soon as I've seen your identification and the paperwork for all of this," Mrs Bryant said flatly.

Doctor Russell reached into her bag and produced a folder full of papers and a shiny plastic identification badge. "No problem. I'd be disappointed if you didn't ask."

Mrs Bryant took the papers. "I didn't *ask*."

Miss Cotton looked away so that nobody saw her smirk at the way the Head had put the doctor down.

***

Mrs Bryant took ten minutes to read Doctor Russell's papers. They seemed perfectly in order but she waited an extra ten minutes before giving the young doctor clearance to carry on. She had told herself it was so that Lucas could at least have a proper lunch. The truth was that she didn't like having her routine upset and she was making a point about who was in charge of Harringden.

"Everything seems to be fine," Mrs Bryant said, handing the papers back to Doctor Russell. "Miss Cotton will take you to Lucas." She held onto the papers for a moment so that both she and Doctor Russell were gripping them. "I expect you to treat my student with care. He's my responsibility while he's here and he is a good lad." She fixed the young doctor with what the students called the 'Bryant Stare'". It had been known to make even the toughest student weak with fear. "You will make this as easy and stress-free for him as you can."

"Of course," Doctor Russell agreed. "This is for his own good to make sure he's doing OK."

Mrs Bryant sniffed. "Miss Cotton, would you take our guest to meet Lucas please?" She turned and walked back into her office without another word.

Doctor Russell puffed her cheeks out as the Head's door closed. "I'm glad she wasn't Head at my school. I'm thirty and I'm terrified of her."

Miss Cotton nodded. "Best way. She doesn't take prisoners where her students' welfare is concerned."

"Quite right." Doctor Russell held out an arm, inviting Miss Cotton to lead the way. "We'd better get a move on or I'll land in detention."

Miss Cotton led the way through the old school corridors towards the canteen. When the place had been a stately home the huge room had been a banqueting hall. Now it was where over a hundred unruly students ate their lunches under the watchful eye of their teachers. On duty at the door was Mr Skinner.

He smiled as he saw Miss Cotton. "Hi." His smiled disappeared when he saw Doctor Russell at Miss Cotton's elbow. "I mean, hello, Miss Cotton."

Miss Cotton tried not to smirk at her boyfriend's terrible effort at hiding their relationship. He had been the same when they started dating. It seemed that everyone knew within a morning. But she didn't mind, really. "This is Doctor Russell," she said. "She's here to see Lucas. And she's not a journalist."

"Good," Mr Skinner smiled. "That's a relief."

Doctor Russell looked back and forth between the teachers in puzzlement. "Should I be a journalist?" she asked. "I thought they were banned here."

"They are," Miss Cotton assured her. "It's…" She waved her hand, dismissing the subject. "It's a private joke."

"Right." Doctor Russell looked none the wiser. "Anyway, I better get on with my work. Can you get Lucas for me?"

"Love to," Mr Skinner said cheerfully. "But he's not here."

Doctor Russell looked at him, confused. "What?"

"Where is he?" Miss Cotton demanded. "Has he finished lunch?"

Mr Skinner shook his head helplessly. "I don't know. He hasn't been here all lunchtime. I thought he might have been sitting out in the grounds but Derek — that's Mr Wheeler — had a look. He wasn't out there. No sign of him at all."

"What if something's happened to him?" Miss Cotton asked.

Mr Skinner squeezed her arm reassuringly. "Don't worry. Jess and Danny aren't here either. They'll be together. They always are. You know them."

Miss Cotton nodded. She was relieved that Lucas wasn't alone. "That's something anyway. We need to find them."

"So where is he likely to be?" Doctor Russell demanded. For the first time her friendly manner had slipped and she sounded annoyed. The two teachers looked at her in surprise. "Sorry," she said. "But I'm on a tight deadline."

Mr Skinner sucked on his bottom lip thoughtfully. "Hard to say. He won't have gone far. Even with that support frame he wears, he struggles to walk a long way."

"So, still in the school, then?" Doctor Russell asked.

"Possibly," Miss Cotton replied. "But…" she paused before continuing. "He wasn't happy about your visit being dropped on him at the last minute. I wonder if he might have gone home?"

"No," Mr Skinner said quickly. "He wouldn't do that. He's a good lad. Mind you," he said thoughtfully. "After the way the last bunch of journalists treated him, if he thought more of them were coming he might have legged it."

"How?" Doctor Russell asked sharply. "He's weak on his legs. "How would he get out of here? There's only one road in to the school grounds."

"One road," Skinner agreed, "but a number of old footpaths. If he was in a bad mood and wanted to get home, he could use one of the paths do it. Especially if the other two were helping him."

"If they've bunked off, they're in so much trouble," Miss Cotton growled. "Still, we'll find out soon enough. Jon — that's Mr Daly, our IT specialist, has gone to the village to find out about the communications outage," she explained to Doctor Russell.

"Has he?" Doctor Russell asked. "When did he go?"

"About ten minutes before you arrived," Miss Cotton answered. "Why?"

Doctor Russell didn't answer. She looked quickly at her watch. "Five minutes to the village," she said to herself. "Twenty in the village, five back here." She was clearly thinking hard and very quickly. Reaching into her bag she pulled out a small hand radio. "Change of plan," she said into the radio. "The target is on the loose. Moving slowly, two companions. Local security forces could be half an hour away. Scout the area — focus on old footpaths. He's slow, so they can't have got far."

"What's that all about?" asked Mr Skinner. "Why did you call Lucas a 'target'?"

"Who are you?" Miss Cotton demanded. "You're not a doctor at all, are you?"

Doctor Russell stuffed the radio into her pocket. "Oh, do shut up," she snapped. When her hand came out of her pocket it was holding a small pistol. "Now, you two are going to answer every question I ask about your precious Martian or this will get very messy."

CHAPTER 4

THE INVADERS

Outside the school's front door, Doctor Russell's two companions sprang to life. Each drew a handgun from their pocket before getting out of the car. They hurried to the white van. Its back door was already opening and eight more men spilled out. With military precision they set off about their tasks. Six of the men hurried out into the grounds. The other four set off to find the school's security guards.

***

"How long till we have to go back?" Danny asked.

Jess checked her watch. "We still have five minutes," she answered.

"Only five minutes?" Lucas grimaced. "Where did lunchtime go?"

"Tell me about it," Jess said. She looked around the little clearing. "It's weird to think somewhere this nice is close to school."

Danny started packing away the wrappers from his lunch. There were more sweet wrappers than anything else. "Do you think we'll get into trouble for going off school grounds?"

"How will they know?" Jess asked.

"You know Bryant," Danny muttered. "She sees everything. It's not normal."

"That's true," Jess admitted. "I think she must have worked for MI5 or something before she came here. She's like Sherlock Holmes — except Sherlock Holmes couldn't give detention." She started clearing up her lunch too.

Lucas was last to begin getting ready to go back to school. "Do you think they'd notice if I just didn't turn up this afternoon?" he asked.

"Yep," Danny answered.

"Totally," Jess agreed.

Lucas looked deeper into the woods. The road to the village was about three hundred metres in that direction. He still had his phone. Miss Cotton had forgotten to tell him to put it back in his locker. If he could get a signal he could call a cab and go home. He thought about it for a moment. He *really* thought about it. But he knew people would be disappointed in him. His friends, his teachers. More than anything, he knew his parents would be upset that he had chosen to run away. He didn't want to disappoint his mum and dad. He turned back to his friends. "Suppose I'd better go back to school, then."

"Yeah," Jess said sadly. "There's no escape."

She took the lead, moving through the thick mix of ferns and grass on the ground. Danny was a few steps behind, with Lucas bringing up the rear some way back.

"So," Jess said, looking back over her shoulder. "Do you think Maya Whitaker really did catch Miss Cotton and Mr Skinner kissing in the science lab?"

"Probably," Danny said. "They…" His voice stopped suddenly. He was staring past Jess, his face swiftly turning grey.

Jess turned around and found herself staring at the nose of a wicked-looking black pistol. She stopped, terrified.

The man holding the gun was dressed in a black top and jeans. He was tall, at least six feet tall, and his face was cold and unemotional. "Where's the Martian?" he demanded flatly.

"I… I…" Jess stammered, trying to find something to say.

"Where is he?" the man demanded again.

"Why have you got a gun?" Danny asked. He seemed unable to take his eyes off the weapon.

"Just tell me where he is," the man repeated. Abruptly, he lurched forward. Jess and Danny threw themselves aside in case the gun went off. The man turned to see Lucas standing with his arm raised. Lucas had seen this stranger threaten his friends and had slipped around behind him, using the trees for cover.

"You're the Martian," the man said. He looked pleased with himself. He lost his smile as a log thumped down on his shoulder. Jess had swung it with all her might. The man spun round towards Jess. Without really thinking, Lucas increased the power setting of his Armour to maximum and he swung his arm at the attacker. The metal of his exo-skeleton hit the man in the chest and sent him sprawling into the grass and ferns, unconscious. Jess and Danny stared at Lucas in shock.

"How did you do that?" Jess asked.

Lucas pointed at his Armour. "Turned it up to twelve," he said.

Jess stared at the unconscious man then picked up his gun and threw it as far away as she could.

"Hey!" Danny protested. "We might need that!"

"Are you going to use it?" Jess demanded. Danny couldn't meet her gaze and looked at the ground. "I didn't think so."

"We need to get back to the school," Lucas said urgently. "We need to let them know about the attack." He pointed at the fallen intruder with disgust. "That's no journalist."

***

"You're not journalists and you're certainly not doctors, so who the devil are you?" Mrs Bryant stood face to face with Jasmine Russell. She gave no hint that she was even slightly intimidated by this woman who had invaded and taken over her school. Even the pistol in Doctor Russell's hand didn't seem to affect her.

"None of your business," Jasmine answered.

"Don't be stupid," the Head snapped. "You have attacked my school and threatened my pupils and staff."

Jasmine took a menacing step towards Mrs Bryant. "And you should be worried about all of your staff and pupils. I am only interested in one."

The Head didn't back down. "What do you want with Lucas?" she demanded.

"Space is big business," Doctor Russell replied. "We have to know how people's bodies will cope with space. When people move to new planets and moons they will want children." She looked at the students with a sour look on her face. "I can't imagine why. But the company that knows most about how kids' bodies cope in space will have a big lead on their rivals. Your Martian, Lucas, is needed for experiments."

"Too bad he's not here," Mrs Bryant said with satisfaction.

"My men will find him," Doctor Russell answered coldly. "Meanwhile, you can wait with the rest."

She pushed the Head towards the door to the dining room. The students and staff had all been herded into that one room and were being guarded by two of Doctor Russell's men. Some of the pupils were crying. The staff looked concerned but were moving among the students trying to reassure them.

"Be quiet, all of you," Doctor Russell shouted loudly. "Silence!" The room slowly hushed and every pair of eyes turned to her. "I have no interest in any of you," she said. "I am only interested in your classmate, Lucas Wilson.

"Once we have him, you will be left alone. So, if any of you know where he is, tell me now. That way we can leave quickly and you can run home to your mummies."

Mrs Bryant's voice cracked through the hall. "Tell this woman nothing." She turned her gaze to her students. "We have no reason to believe her. All we know is that she has lied and wants to hurt one of our pupils."

"I've had enough of you." Doctor Russell grabbed Mrs Bryant by the arm and hauled her away towards the door. The Head struggled but couldn't break free of the younger woman's iron grip.

"Get off me!" she cried.

"Find a very small cupboard and lock her in it," Doctor Russell said to one of her men. He nodded and dragged the Head out of the room. "Now," Doctor Russell said to the students and staff. "Your Head obviously isn't in charge here

anymore. I am. So… where is the Martian boy?"
She looked around. "The best way for you all to
be safe is to tell me."

Everyone started to look around the room,
wondering if anybody knew what had happened
to Lucas, wondering if anyone would give up
a student to this awful woman. They all looked
around uncertainly, not sure of what was going
to happen. Nobody spoke or moved for a long
moment and then a voice came from the back of
the hall."

"I saw them."

Everyone turned and looked at James Gossford,
who was slowly making his way through the
crowd. The students moved aside to let James
Gossford pass.

"Gossford, keep quiet," Miss Cotton said loudly.
Immediately, one of Doctor Russell's men took
a step towards her, and Mr Skinner pulled Miss
Cotton back.

"At last," Doctor Russell said, looking at Gossford. "One of you has the sense to do what's best for all of you. Where is he?" she asked Gossford.

"I was in detention at the back of the school," Gossford said. He sounded nervous. He looked nervous too.

"And?" Doctor Russell demanded.

"I saw the Martian and his friends hurrying away into the woods." He pointed over his shoulder "That way."

"When?"

"Start of lunch," Gossford answered quickly. "They were running," he added when he saw anger filling Doctor Russell's face.

Doctor Russell strode towards Miss Cotton. "Where would they go?" she demanded.

"I don't know," the teacher answered.

"Would you still not know if I threatened your boyfriend?"

"No, I wouldn't," Miss Cotton answered angrily. "And don't you even think of threatening him."

Doctor Russell looked at her, amused, for a moment. "Do all the teachers here have such a big mouth?" she sneered. "Bring him," she said to one of her men, pointing a finger at Gossford.

"What?" Gossford spluttered. "You said…"

Doctor Russell spun and strode to Gossford so that her face was only centimetres from his. "I said you would all go free when I had the Martian. For all I know you lied to help him get away."

"I wouldn't do that," Gossford protested. "I can't stand the freak."

"So you say." Doctor Russell wasn't convinced. "So you're with us until we have the precious Lucas."

When they had escaped for their picnic lunch, Lucas and his friends had run across the two hundred metres of open ground as fast as they could. Coming back, they had to do exactly the same. This time they ran even faster, and with his Armour still at maximum, Lucas led the way.

As soon as they entered the school they all knew something was wrong. There were no students or teachers around. The office was abandoned, too, and that was something that never happened.

"Mrs Bryant never leaves the reception area unattended," Jess said.

They looked into the Head's office and found it empty as well. Jess indicated the technician's office and they quickly went inside, closing the door behind them.

"Something's definitely wrong here," Danny said.

"You're right." Jess had the phone to her ear. The phone line is still dead. How about your mobile, Lucas?"

"There was no signal a few minutes ago. Everything is still down." Lucas was standing by the window, peering out. He made sure he was out of sight of anyone looking at the window. "But it's worse than that," he said. He sounded worried and he knew it. His friends joined him. Out in the grounds they could see two men dressed in the same manner as the man who had attacked them in the woods.

"They must have taken over the school," Danny whispered.

"Looks like it," Jess agreed.

"There's another one," Lucas said quietly. Sure enough, a third man was approaching the pair in the grounds. It took them a moment to realise that it was the one Lucas had knocked out. He was walking with a bad limp but he was awake. "We're in trouble now," Lucas whispered.

Jess held up a finger to her lips. A moment later they heard voices outside. One was female, the other familiar and unwelcome.

"But I wouldn't try to help Lucas." The whining voice was unmistakably James Gossford's. "I can't stand him or his creepy friends."

"Good." The woman sounded bored by Gossford's moaning. "Then you won't have lied to me and you can go free unharmed."

The voices moved away so that their words became muffled and unclear before fading.

"They've *definitely* taken the school," Lucas said.

Jess was still standing near the door, listening. "Pity we've no idea who 'they' are," she said.

"It's not all bad," Danny muttered. "They've taken Gossford prisoner. Maybe they'll keep him."

Jess glared at her friend. "This isn't the time for jokes — even though I can't stand Gossford either."

"We can't stay in here," Lucas said softly. "If they're moving around outside they'll look in here sooner or later."

Jess agreed. "But where can we go?" she asked. "If they have the whole school…"

Danny interrupted. "There are bits of the school we know that they don't. It's an old building."

"The cellars?" suggested Jess. "Nobody ever goes down there."

"Because the doors are always locked," Lucas answered.

"Not all of them," Danny explained quickly. "The caretaker's office has a door to the cellar. I think his office used to be a room where servants got stuff ready."

Jess waved a hand to silence her friend. "The history lesson can wait till later," she said. "All we need to do is get to the caretaker's office."

Danny nodded. "It's not far. Just along the corridor. We could be there in half a minute."

They all looked at each other, thinking of any objections to this plan. There were none.

"OK," Lucas said. "We go to the caretaker's office and then hide out in the cellars."

"They're like a rabbit warren," Danny said. "Nobody will find us down there."

Jess lifted a hand in front of Danny's face for quiet. "Ssssh!" She tilted her head, listening at the door. "Somebody's coming."

A few seconds later Lucas and Danny could hear men's voices outside in the corridor. The voices were muffled by the door but the conversation could be heard clearly.

"You have Doctor Russell's orders," one of the men said. "Get to it."

"Right," the other man replied.

The three friends looked at each other. They were all wondering who this Doctor Russell person was — and what their orders might be. Whatever the orders were, they were bound to be bad for them.

The orders became clear very quickly. From the corridor they heard the sound of a door being thrown open. Moments later they heard heavy footsteps moving closer to their hiding place. The footsteps stopped and the door handle started to move.

CHAPTER 5

HIDING PLACE

Lucas moved quickly across the room. He put his arm under the door handle. When the man outside pushed down on the handle on his side of the door, the handle on the other side was stopped from moving by Lucas's Armour. The man outside tried again. The handle still refused to move. The pressure on the door handle stopped. Lucas and his friends heard the sound of heavy, booted feet moving away. Lucas stayed in that position for a few minutes in case the man came back. Eventually they relaxed slightly. The man outside seemed to have gone — but they knew there was only one way to be sure of that.

Lucas slowly moved his arm away from under the door handle. Very gently, he pushed the handle down and pulled the door open a fraction. He opened it a little further and peered out into the corridor. He looked back at his friends. "It's clear," he said. "Whoever that was, he's gone."

"Are we still going to the cellar?" Danny asked. He looked genuinely scared. "I mean, they've tried this door. They won't come back here." He looked hopefully at his friends. "Will they?"

Jess pointed at the window. "This is the ground floor, Danny. They only have to look in the window and we'll be caught."

"I suppose so," Danny conceded.

"It's not far to the caretaker's office," Lucas reassured his friend. "We'll be safe when we get there. We just need to be quick and quiet."

They ran along the corridor and stopped where it turned sharply to the left. Jess peeked round the corner.

"Nobody there," she whispered.

All three ran for the nearest door, which was marked CARETAKER. They were relieved that it was open, and all three hurried inside. Danny pulled the door closed behind them.

"Where is the door to the cellar?" Lucas asked.

Jess led her friends across the caretaker's office. A set of wooden railings ran out from the wall. Behind the railings, a set of old stone steps led down to a door. "There it is," Jess said. "A few of us came down here for a project last year."

"And it was horrible and scary," Danny said. "It's all dark and full of cobwebs."

"But it's not as scary as men with guns," Jess added.

Danny had to agree with that. "There's a really good place down here. There's a wall that has a gap in it."

"We'll be safe if we get through that," Jess agreed.

Lucas led the way down the stairs with his friends close behind him. He pulled the door open... and found himself looking into the surprised face of one of the men who had invaded the school. It was the same man Lucas had knocked out in the woods. The man looked back at Lucas with an equal amount of surprise on his face. It faded quickly and he charged for the door.

"You!" the man bellowed.

Out of reflex, Lucas slammed the door. There was a dull thump as the running man hit the door hard. A second later there was the sound of another thud in the cellar as the man hit the floor. Lucas cautiously pulled the door open again. The man was sprawled on the cellar floor, unconscious again.

"It's the same guy," Jess said. "And you've knocked him out cold again."

Danny smiled at Lucas. "He's really going to hate you when he wakes up."

"I'm not very fond of him either," Lucas answered. He pushed the cellar door closed and turned the key in the lock. "OK," he said, leading the way back up the steps. "We need somewhere else to hide now that we can't go in the cellar. He threw the cellar door key into a dark corner of the room.

Danny offered a suggestion. "There are other places here to hide, especially on the first floor."

"If we can get up to the first floor," Lucas said. He pointed a thumb at the cellar door to indicate that he was talking about the man he had knocked out. "We don't know how many of them there are."

"True. We'd have to use the side stairs," Jess said thoughtfully. The main staircase is too open."

"All right," Lucas said. "We'll do that."

They waited, listening at the door, to make sure there was nobody near. When they were sure that it was safe, they slipped into the corridor. Jess led the way. She took them on a roundabout route, avoiding the main corridors. At one point they stopped when she held up a hand. They were ready to hide inside the nearest classroom but Jess waved her hand. "It's OK," she whispered. Ten metres further ahead they turned a corner and found themselves in the corridor leading to the smaller stairs. These had been the servants' stairs when the building had belonged to a wealthy family. In those days the owners and their servants didn't mix together. Lucas had never understood how people living in the same house could have been treated so differently. However, this really wasn't the time to think about that. Getting to safety was what mattered.

"Come on," Lucas said to his friends.

They were halfway to the stairs when they heard a door being shaken violently. They stopped and looked around desperately. They needed to get out of sight but there were no classrooms to hide in.

"Open this door!"

"Wait," Jess said. "I know that voice."

"Let me out of here," a woman's voice yelled from behind the only door on the corridor. They all recognised it immediately.

"Mrs Bryant?" Danny asked. "What's she doing in the cleaner's cupboard?"

Lucas took a step towards the door. "Let's find out." He brought his arm down hard, smashing the metal plates of his Armour against the door handle and lock. They shattered and he pulled the door open. The Head looked out. She seemed shocked by the identity of her rescuers.

"Lucas?" she said softly. "What are you doing?" She looked around nervously. "You need to get out of sight. These people are here to get you. You can't let them see you."

"We know they're here for Lucas," Jess said. "We've avoided being caught so far."

"Only just," Danny added.

"Yeah," Jess agreed. "Only just."

"Who are those men?" Lucas asked. "And who's the woman who took Gossford?"

"Gossford?" The Head asked. "What's he got to do with it?" She shook her head. "Never mind that for now. We need to get you to somewhere safe."

"That's what we were planning when we heard you," Lucas answered.

The Head was still looking around nervously. "We need to get there quickly. They'll be back to check on me before long."

"Jess?" Lucas looked at his friend.

"This way," Jess answered.

With Jess in the lead, all four hurried towards the back stairs.

***

James Gossford was terrified.

For the first time in his life he realised that all his parents' money and influence weren't going to get him out of the trouble he was in — and that fear made him shake.

The woman — Jasmine Russell — was taking a report from a large man who was nursing an aching neck and head.

"You didn't see which way he went?" she asked the man.

"No, but there were no tracks leading out through the woods. Only back here."

At that moment another of her men had arrived and reported that the Head had broken out of the cupboard she had been locked in.

"The lock was smashed?" Doctor Russell said. "On the outside? That means somebody broke her out… it has to be the Martian." She smiled. James Gossford thought that even though Doctor Russell was a very pretty woman, there was something really unpleasant about her smile. "That means he's in the school," she said. "The idiot's come back. Find him and bring him to me." She pushed her stooge hard in the chest. *"Find him now!"*

***

"And how long have you known about this place?" Mrs Bryant demanded of her three pupils. "I've been here for nearly ten years and I had no idea it was here."

They were in a small, narrow room. It was lit only by daylight streaming through a small window high on one of the walls. The only furnishings were a few battered, hard old chairs. The door to the room was hidden on the outside, appearing to be part of the antique wooden panelling in that part of the school. Around two metres up, at the top of one of the panels, there was a small catch that released the door.

"It's the Geeks' Hideaway," Jess explained. "If we need somewhere to hide out from people like Gossford, this is where we come. It's been kind of a secret among, well, the *less cool* students, for years." She looked at her friends. "Sorry, but that's us."

"Thanks a lot," Danny grumbled. "So, we've got maniacs running around the school and on top of that, we're not cool."

"Having this place makes you *very* cool," Mrs Bryant assured Danny. She looked at the battered old shelves on one of the walls. "This must have been a storage room for the servants. They would keep stuff in here rather than lug it up and down the stairs all the time." She shook her head with irritation. "And if you ever tell anyone I used the word 'stuff' like that, you are all in trouble."

"Our lips are zipped," Jess promised.

The little bit of banter relaxed Lucas a little, but he still needed to know what would happen next. "What are we going to do?" he asked.

"Not a thing," Mrs Bryant answered quickly. "I sent Mr Daly into the village. I told him to check in at the police station to see if they knew what was happening. I also asked him to contact your mother while he was at the police station. When she tells them that she didn't agree to a doctor visiting you today, they will come here to see what is going on. The police will be here before long. They'll deal with it better than we can."

Lucas nodded and sank onto one of the chairs. It creaked under his weight. "Suits me."

Mrs Bryant moved the other chair to the wall just under the window and leaped up onto it.

She was quite athletic for someone in her forties, Lucas thought.

The Head was standing on her tiptoes. Even like that she could only just see out of the very bottom of the window. "Why couldn't I have been taller?" she muttered. She spoke again. This time she was talking to her three students. "I can see the grounds here but not the driveway." She dropped lightly back to the floor. "So," she said. "It looks like we just have to wait until we hear the police sirens."

"OK," Jess agreed.

"I'm glad you were suspicious.' Lucas said.

Mrs Bryant looked around the little room. "Now, I don't suppose you keep anything interesting in here we can do to pass the time?"

A voice sounded from outside in the corridor, but it was louder than a natural voice should be and it seemed to echo. It took a second to realise that the voice was using the school's public address system. "Lucas Wilson, we know you're in the school."

Mrs Bryant laid a supportive hand on Lucas's shoulder. "They'll have guessed it was you who broke me out of jail," she said. "She's just guessing that you're still here in school."

The voice continued outside. "We have over a hundred of your fellow students and teachers held prisoner. If you give yourself up to us, none of them will be hurt. If you don't…" the voice trailed off menacingly. "You have five minutes to come to the reception area or it's going to be very bad for one of the students or teachers here." She paused viciously. "*Very* nasty."

CHAPTER 6

JAILBREAK

Before Jasmine Russell had stopped speaking, Lucas started to stand.

Mrs Bryant's hand pushed down on Lucas's shoulder. "Don't even think about it. They're holding everyone in the dining hall. They know they only have a few minutes before the police get here. You just have to wait here till then."

"What do you mean *I* have to wait?" Lucas asked, wondering why the Head was making for the door.

"Not just you, Lucas," Mrs Bryant smiled back. "Jess and Danny are staying, too. I just need to keep that woman and her thugs occupied until the police get here," she said. "Stay here, all of you." The Head quickly pulled the catch to release the door and slipped out into the corridor. The door closed behind her with a little click.

Lucas and his friends looked at each other for a long moment.

"So we just sit here?" Jess asked finally.

"Suits me," Danny answered. "Those people out there are dangerous."

"And Mrs Bryant just went to hold them up on her own," Jess replied quickly.

"That was her decision," Danny answered. "I didn't want her to go either but we couldn't stop her." He shrugged in frustration. "What can we do?"

Lucas stood up rapidly. "We can get the rest of the students out of the school," he said.

"What?" Danny squeaked. He looked at Lucas as if his friend had gone mad.

Lucas smiled encouragingly at his friends. "If that Doctor Russell woman is waiting for us in the reception area, she'll have most of her men there, right?"

"So?" Jess asked.

Lucas was excited. He obviously had a plan. "That means we can get everybody out a different way."

Jess was interested but had no idea how Lucas planned to do this. "How?" she asked. "When Mrs Bryant comes down the stairs they'll know we're up here somewhere. They're bound to come looking for us."

"I know," Lucas agreed eagerly. "That's why we shouldn't be here. Come on."

Lucas listened at the door before he pulled it door open. He hurried out. Jess and Danny ran after him. There wasn't really anything else they could have done. He was their best friend.

"So how do we get away from here?" Jess asked. "They will be watching all the staircases by now."

Lucas looked towards the stairs and then moved instead to the history classroom opposite. He pushed the door open and ran to the window. He looked out, scanning the grounds below.

"Nobody there," he said, pulling the window open.

"So?" Danny asked. "What's that got to do with anything? And what are you doing?" he squealed as Lucas pulled himself up onto the windowsill.

Lucas beamed at his friends and held his arms out wide. "We don't need to use the stairs."

Danny took a step backwards. Jess bit on her lip thoughtfully. "Your Armour," she said to Lucas. "Can it handle all of our weight?"

"I think so." Lucas agreed.

Danny had gone very pale. "You think so?" he said. "You mean you're not sure?"

"Not totally sure," Lucas admitted.

"Couldn't you have just lied and said you were absolutely certain?" Danny fretted.

Jess thought for a moment then ran over to join Lucas. "All right. I'll trust you."

Danny stood at the door, looking back at the corridor and then at his friends. "Oh, all right," he said finally. "But this is a terrible idea."

The sound of booted feet running on wooden floors made up their minds. "Staying here is a worse idea," Jess said.

Both Jess and Danny climbed up beside Lucas. Just inside the window, Danny clung to one side of Lucas and Jess to the other. They both put their feet on the solid metal plates covering his feet.

The footsteps in the corridor were coming closer.

Lucas tightened his grip on his friends. "Ready?"

"No," Danny replied.

"Good," Lucas smiled and he stepped through the open window. The drop was between three and four metres and they fell quickly. To everyone's amazement, Lucas landed firmly on his feet. The Armour was still turned up to maximum and easily took the stresses of the landing.

"Nothing's broken," Danny said, sounding shocked.

Lucas waved his Armour under Danny's chin. "Told you." He turned and looked around, making sure there were none of Doctor Russell's guards in the area. They ran to one of the hidden, set-back areas of the building, out of view from the front. A moment later they heard the history classroom window creak open as one of Doctor Russell's men looked out.

"Nothing here," they heard the man say. "It's just an open window." A second later the window slammed shut.

Jess caught Lucas by the arm to stop him moving. "Wait a minute," she said. "Just in case he looks out again."

They waited a long moment before Jess relaxed and nodded.

"OK," Lucas said. "He's not coming back. Let's move." They hurried along the side of the school, sticking close to the wall. The three stopped about ten metres along the wall and carefully peered through the window. Inside they could see the students and teachers gathered in the dining room. They all looked worried and frightened.

Looking around the room Lucas could make out two of Doctor Russell's guards by the door. They were both big men but neither looked very bright. They were watching the students and teachers. Their eyes never moved towards the windows. He gripped the edge of the window and pushed upwards. To begin with it didn't move but Lucas increased pressure. He felt that he had more control over his Armour now. Slowly, the window began sliding upwards. Lucas lifted a finger to his lips to silence the nearest student inside. Moving to the side, Lucas opened a second window. From here he had a better view of the two men guarding the students. They both looked vicious but they hadn't seen him. That was what mattered.

At Lucas's feet were half a dozen large plant pots, which the groundsman tended with care. The groundsman loved to have flowers on show in summer. The pots were heavy but with his Armour at full power they were almost as light as air. Pulling his arm back, Lucas hurled one of the pots in through the open window. It flew through the air and smashed into one of the guards. It hit him hard in the chest and knocked him to the ground. By the time the second guard realised what had happened and had looked up to see where the attack was coming from, all he had time to see was the second plant pot flying at him. An instant later the plant pot slammed into him hard. It exploded in a mess of compost and fragments of the clay pot. He dropped to the floor beside his friend. They were both unconscious.

Mr Skinner and Miss Cotton were the first to move, scooping up the guns dropped by the guards. Neither looked comfortable handling the weapons. While Mr Skinner stayed on guard at the door, Miss Cotton ran across to the window. She had a mixture of emotions on her face. She was relieved to see Lucas and his friends but she was also confused and very concerned.

"Lucas?" said Miss Cotton. Are you all right?"

"We're fine," Lucas answered.

"For now," Danny added, looking around nervously.

"What's going on?" Miss Cotton asked.

Lucas quickly explained. "Mrs Bryant went to keep them busy. We were supposed to hide but…" his voice tailed off.

"But we didn't," Jess interrupted.

Lucas smiled at his friend and continued. "We're getting everybody out through the windows." He pointed over his shoulder at the trees a few hundred metres away. "They can get into the woods and hide there."

"Or use one of the paths to get to the village," suggested Jess.

Miss Cotton squeezed Lucas and Jess's arms. "I'm proud of all three of you," she said. The young teacher turned to the students, who were all staring at the window in confusion. "Right, everyone. We're getting out of here."

Under strict instructions to move quietly, the students opened all of the dining-room windows and climbed out. With teachers taking the lead and bringing up the rear, the students ran across the open ground for the woods. Last out were Miss Cotton and Mr Skinner. They had gagged and tied up the unconscious guards with rope from the caretaker's office before climbing out of the windows. Neither of the teachers seemed eager to leave for some reason. It took Lucas a moment to understand why they didn't want to go. "Is it about Mrs Bryant?" he asked.

Mr Skinner nodded. "That Doctor Russell woman who is holding her is vicious. She's going to go wild when she finds everybody has escaped from here."

"I just don't know how we can help her," Miss Cotton said helplessly.

At that moment they all heard a distant wailing sound. "Sirens," Mr Skinner said quickly. "Come on." He led them away from the window and along the side of the school building. Lucas became aware that Jess and Danny were still with them, too.

"Why didn't you two go with the others?" he demanded.

"Why didn't *you*?" Jess asked. "You're the one they're after!"

Lucas didn't have an answer for that. He shrugged. "I hadn't thought that far ahead, I suppose."

They had reached the corner of the school building. Peering round the corner they could see the car and van that had brought the invaders to the school. Back along the path they saw police cars and vans turning into the school's long drive. A chime came from Lucas's pocket. He checked his phone. He had four bars showing a strong signal. "My phone's got a signal."

The police cars suddenly screeched to a halt and began reversing back to the school gates.

"What on earth?" asked Miss Cotton.

The reason for the police's sudden reverse was explained when the school doors opened and Mrs Bryant, along with a terrified-looking James Gossford, were pushed out in front of the phoney Doctor Russell and what remained of her men. Doctor Russell had a phone to her ear and her voice carried clearly to Lucas and his friends.

"Yes, we have hostages," Doctor Russell said. "And if you try to stop us leaving… well, it will be a bad day for them. A *very*, *very* bad day."

CHAPTER 7

THE HERO

Nobody who had heard Jasmine Russell's threats against Mrs Bryant and Gossford doubted that she meant every single word.

Mr Skinner pushed Miss Cotton and his three students back a little. It was a reflex action. He just wanted to keep them safe.

They all watched Mrs Bryant and Gossford being pushed into the back of the car with Doctor Russell and one of her men. The rest of the intruders clambered into the van. Moments later, the car was moving along the drive.

"Do you think the police will let them go?" Danny asked.

The answer came with a quick set of dull bangs. "The car tyres," Miss Cotton said.

"It's where the police cars got to before they turned back," Mr Skinner said thoughtfully. "They must have dropped something to burst those tyres."

"Sneaky," Danny said. He definitely approved. "I like it."

"I bet it was a stinger," Jess said. "It's like a long metal chain with spikes on it," she explained. "I saw it online."

Doctor Russell's car struggled to continue going straight ahead. Its nose weaved around violently. The car skidded sideways and came to a halt at the side of the path. The van, which was heavier and had more momentum, couldn't stop as quickly. It swerved off the drive and clipped a tree on the side of the little road. Hitting the tree made the van spin and skid along sideways for a few metres. By chance, the van blocked the view to the car from the police's position. Doctor Russell must have noticed that she was hidden from the view of the police. Very quickly she was out of the car and running, pushing Gossford and Mrs Bryant ahead of her.

Mrs Bryant was clearly moving as slowly as she could. They saw Doctor Russell prod her in the back. Mrs Bryant stumbled and ran on.

Jess had worked out Doctor Russell's plan. "She's making for the woods," she said.

She was right. Jasmine Russell was hurrying her captives towards the line of trees. "If she gets in there, they might lose her," Mr Skinner said. He started running after Doctor Russell.

"Dave, don't!" Miss Cotton called after Mr Skinner but it was too late. He was already sprinting. "He'll never get there in time."

Lucas was sprinting. He didn't remember making the decision to run. It just happened. It was what needed to happen and so he just did it. He didn't stop to think. *He just did it.* With his Armour at full power he ran faster than any boy could. He probably ran faster than any human had ever run before. He passed Mr Skinner within seconds and was running towards Jasmine Russell and her prisoners. The more he relaxed, the faster he ran. For the first time, Lucas felt really at home in his Armour. He liked the way it let him run. He liked the speed it gave him. He liked the strength it gave him. It helped him to feel like he belonged in his own body. He ran even faster.

Lucas heard Mr Skinner's voice from behind him. The teacher was shouting. Up ahead, Lucas saw Jasmine Russell turn. She stared in shock at Lucas as he hurtled towards her. Gathering all his energy and speed, Lucas leaped at Doctor Russell. He had aimed to go just over her head but she dropped to the ground in fear. He flew well over her head. The leap felt so natural to Lucas. It was as if he was home on Mars with its lower gravity. But even on Mars his leaps hadn't been quite this good.

Lucas didn't want the leap to ever stop but he came down about ten metres beyond Doctor Russell. He landed easily on his feet. When he turned he saw Mr Skinner rugby tackle her. It was a really solid hit. She had just got back to her feet when Mr Skinner had tackled her and knocked the dreadful woman back to the ground. Mrs Bryant ran back to help Mr Skinner. Within a few seconds they had used one of Mr Skinner's large handkerchiefs to tie Doctor Russell's hands behind her back.

Mrs Bryant scooped up the fallen gun and aimed it at Jasmine Russell. Lucas knew his head teacher could never use the pistol. She hated violence. He was also sure that Doctor Russell wouldn't know that fact. Mrs Bryant certainly looked angry enough to terrify the woman.

"Nobody comes into my school and threatens my students," the Head said coldly.

A police car was speeding across the grass towards them. Other police cars had already surrounded the van. The car drew up a few metres from Lucas and a group of police officers jumped out. Doctor Russell was quickly put in handcuffs and pushed into the back of the police car. One of the officers took the pistol from Mrs Bryant. She looked relieved to have the horrible thing taken from her.

Two of the police officers drove Jasmine Russell away. She glared at both Lucas and Mrs Bryant with real hatred. Lucas didn't care. What mattered was that the woman was in handcuffs. She would soon be in jail. He hoped she would spend a lot of time in prison for what she had done.

The remaining officers led Lucas, Mrs Bryant, Mr Skinner and a very quiet James Gossford back to the school. Everyone was going to have to give statements. On the way back, Gossford made a statement of his own to Lucas.

"I'm sorry I told them where you went," Gossford said miserably. "It's going to look bad for me. When everybody tells the police I sold you out but you still came after us to help. So… I'm sorry."

Lucas didn't have the heart to say he had really only done it to help Mrs Bryant and Mr Skinner. Gossford hadn't really been in his thoughts at all. "Fair enough," he said.

That was the end of their conversation. Neither boy had anything else to say.

At the school, Jess and Danny gave Lucas a huge hug. So did Miss Cotton — but only after she had hugged Mr Skinner first.

"You looked like you were flying," Jess said. She sounded so excited.

"It *felt* like I was flying," Lucas laughed.

"When we give our statements, the police will want to know everything," she added.

"Everything?" Lucas asked. "That means Mrs Bryant will find out we went out of school and into the woods for lunch."

"I already know," the Head said from behind them, making all three jump in surprise. "But I'll let you off… just this once."

***

Before Lucas could give his statement, his mother arrived at the school. She fussed over him as mothers do and said she wanted to take him home straight away. Lucas surprised her by refusing.

"I want to stay," he said.

"Are you sure?" Mum asked.

"Yes," Lucas nodded. "I have to give my statement."

That was only part of the reason. Along with Jess and Danny, Lucas had received thanks and congratulations from a lot of the other students. Everyone in school was grateful for what they had done. For the first time he felt accepted by all the other pupils and he wanted to share that moment with his friends.

Nobody was calling him a freak any more.
A couple of people even called him a hero.

For the first time since he had arrived on Earth, Lucas didn't feel like an alien.

THE END

ABOUT THE AUTHOR

Iain McLaughlin lives in his hometown of Dundee in Scotland, in a house filled with books. He has written more than a dozen novels and around fifty plays for radio or audio, many about popular characters and series including James Bond, Doctor Who and Sherlock Holmes. For a time he was the editor of the *Beano* comic.